characters crea

lauren child

This
is ACTUALLY
my
Party

PUFFIN

Charlie and Lola ™

Text based on script Dave Ingham

Written by

Illustrations from the TV animation produced by Tiger Aspect

PUFFIN BOOKS
Published by the Penguin Group: London, New York, Australia,
Canada, India, Ireland, New Zealand and South Africa
Penguin Books Ltd, Registered Offices: 80 Strand, London WC2R 0RL, England

puffinbooks.com

First published 2007
Published in this edition 2011
1 3 5 7 9 10 8 6 4 2
Text and illustrations copyright © Lauren Child/Tiger Aspect Productions Limited, 2007
The Charlie and Lola logo is a trademark of Lauren Child
Made and printed in China
ISBN: 978-0-141-33374-8

I have this little sister Lola.
She is small and very funny.
Today is my birthday, and I'm having a party.
All my friends are invited.
All my friends and Lola!

"Look at all your **birthday cards**, Charlie..."

"Lola!" I say.
"You opened MY cards!"

And Lola says,
"I know, but Mum said I should help
make sure you have an
EXTREMELY lovely happy birthday.

That's why I helped you
open your cards."

"There's going
     to be lots
of **presents**..."
     says Lola.

"Oh, I can't wait!
     I can't wait!"

"And lots of party games.

Like musical statues!"

"And of course the cake!
I love
birthday parties!"
says Lola.   "Oh, I can't wait!
I can't wait!"

Then I say,
"Well, my party's not going
to be quite like that, Lola...

...because LOOK!
Mum has made me
a special **cake**
because MY party is
a **monster** party."

Lola says,
"It's a shame there's
no **pink** icing."

I say,
"That's because
it's a **monster cake**
and **monsters**
hate **pink**."

When everything is ready,
Dad says he'll take me to the shops,
to get my own **scary** mask.

I say to Lola,
"Do you want
to come too?"

Lola says,
"No thank you,
Charlie.

I'm going to help
Mum make more
party things."

"Pink is definitely for **p**ar**t**ie**s**!

Yes,

pin**k**,

pin**k**,

pin**k**.

Charlie's
going to be
SO pleased."

When I get back from the shops,
we put on our **party** costumes
and wait for my friends to arrive.

Then we hear a knock
at the door.

"I'll get it," says Lola

I say,
"Wow, thanks for
coming, everyone!
We've got **monster** drinks.
Come on in!"

But then Lola says,
"Look at Marv's present,
Charlie!

It's
a
TELESPOKE!"

"Lola!" I say.
"Please let ME unwrap
MY **presents** myself."

And Lola says,
"OK, Charlie,
    I'm just helping."

Then I say,
"My dad's made up all these
games for us
in the garden.

There's **monster** tag,
and
monster chase..."

"Musical statues, everyone!"
says Lola.

"Ready,

steady,

GO!"

"No musical statues, Lola.
We're going to play MY **monster** games outside."

Then Marv says,
"Are we going to have any **cake**?"
And I say,
"Oh yes, wait till you see it!"

"Happy birthday, Charlie!

Lola says,
"I just like parties."

"I know you like parties, Lola. But this is actually my party."

Lola says,
"I'm sorry."

And I say,
"Well, at least you didn't give anyone pink fairy cakes."

Then we go to play monster tag outside.

"Charlie, Charlie! Release me, before the Frankenstein gets me!"

And... and... FOUR...
You blow out my candles!

This is
my party,
not your party!"

Lola says,
"What's wrong, Charlie?"

So I say,
    "ONE.
You open all my cards.

TWO.
You open my present from Marv.

THREE.
You make everyone
play YOUR
party games.

ONE...

   TWO...

THREE..."

"Oops!
   Happy birthday,
Charlie!"

While we are playing **monster** tag,
Lola has an idea...

"Monsters,
monsters,
monsters."

When we go back inside…

...Lola has made **monster**
party bags for all my friends!
Lola says, "Thank you for
coming to Charlie's party."

Then Marv sees Lola's fairy cakes.
"Oh, can I have one of those?"

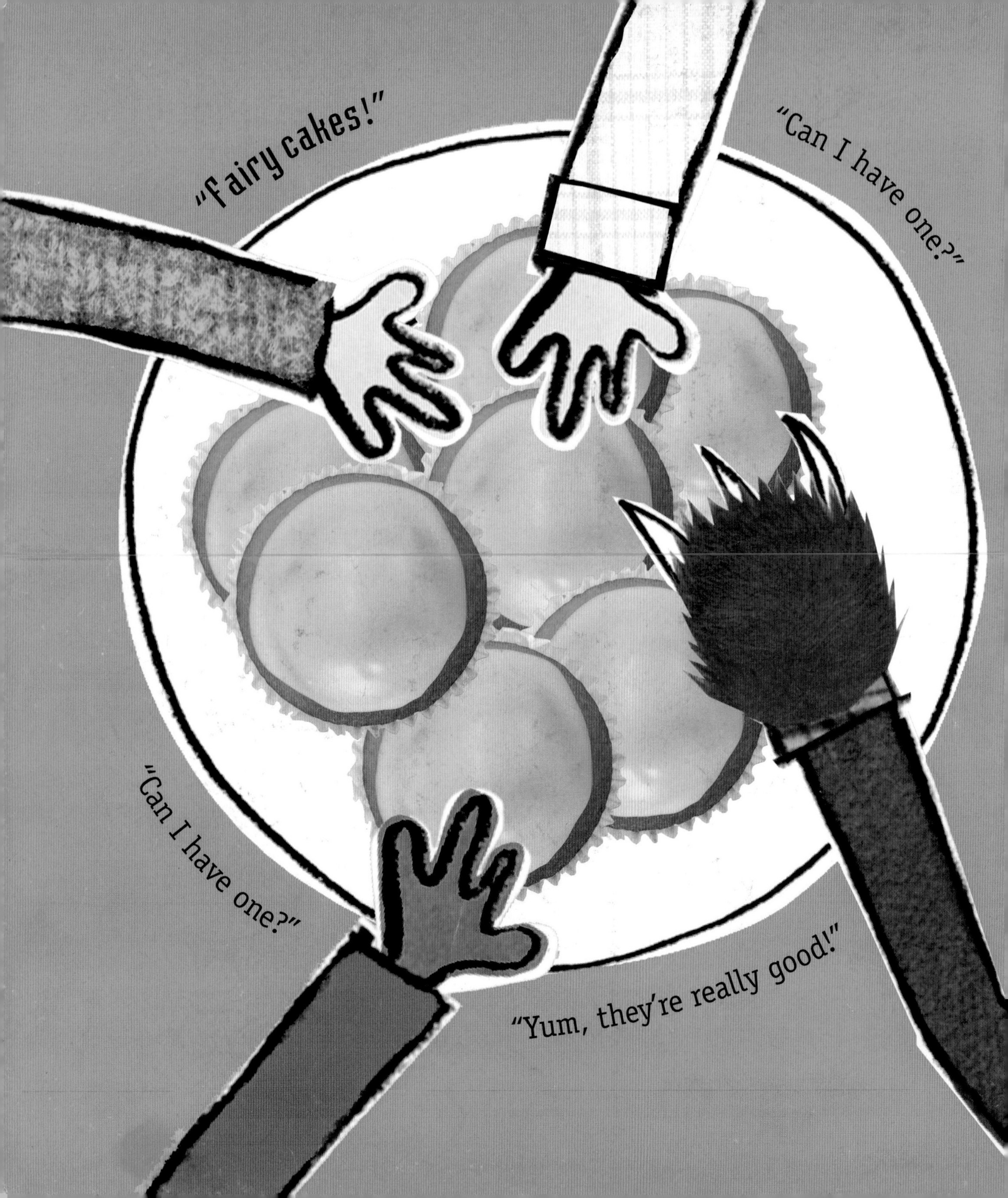
"Fairy cakes!"
"Can I have one?"
"Can I have one?"
"Yum, they're really good!"

And Marv says,
"Thank you, Lola.
Pink icing is really tasty."

Later, Lola says,
"That was a REALLY good party, wasn't it?"
                And I say, "That was a REALLY good party."
Lola says, "They REALLY liked my pink fairy cakes!"
                And I say,
"Even monsters think pink icing is the tastiest!"